Huckleberry

By

Parisa Jenkins

© Parisa Jenkins 2024

All rights reserved, including the right to reproduce this book, or portions thereof in any form. No part of this text may be reproduced, transmitted, downloaded, decompiled, reverse engineered, or stored, in any form or introduced into any information storage and retrieval system, in any form or by any means, whether electronic or mechanical without the express written permission of the author.

ISBN: 978-1-917129-64-0

Prologue
"Tiny Moves"

This book is dedicated to Ann Greenwood. She was my mentor, my teacher but most of all my dear friend. She offered me guidance, friendship and support on pretty much a daily basis for many years. This book is inspired by her and her love of animals; something that we both shared.

She rather generously gifted her beloved Friesian horse Gertsje (pronounced Gertsy) to me five and a half years ago when she was no longer able to ride her due to health issues. Here is the public thank you that I wrote to her.

"There are no words I can use to describe how privileged I feel to be welcoming this amazing girl into my life. I've loved her from afar for a few years now. She belongs to a very dear friend of mine and will always be hers however, quite fantastically, and I can't believe I'm writing this, my friend has, due to her own personal struggles and circumstances agreed to permanently loan her to me. I've promised that I will love and care for this beautiful mare to the best of my ability. She owns a piece of my heart already and I'm excited about the adventure we are about to embark on together. Welcome home Gertsje. I'll hold your hand every step of the way."

Ann died a few months ago. It wasn't unexpectedly but it felt hard to swallow. It still does. Those who know me are aware that I've suffered several losses in my life. I've found them all difficult to deal with and carry but this one, so far, is the hardest. I'm told my struggle to cope mentally is probably due to a culmination of trauma when it comes to personal loss. Maybe.

At the moment, writing and thinking about Ann makes me feel really quite unwell. It's a feeling I don't enjoy but I don't want to not think or write about her. She was a huge part of my life that I want to remember. Is the price we pay for love inconsolable and unbearable grief? If so, how is that fair?

I have been told there is always a positive somewhere but that sometimes it can be hard to find. The positive of losing Ann is that it has pushed me back into writing after a three-year break. Putting pen to paper seems to help me cope with grief, albeit temporarily. Music also seems to help me a bit too, which is why every chapter of this book is named after an appropriate song. Tiny moves in the right direction, hopefully.

Ann read all of my books and loved every one of them. She kindly told me that I wrote very well and that I should be proud of myself. She said that each book was even better than the previous one she had read. She read them in sequence of them being written. So, according to her wisdom, this one should be absolutely terrific.

When I eventually finish this book (however long that takes me) I'll imagine her saying rather genuinely, "It's just brilliant, love, the best one so far." My ramblings in this book are therefore all Ann's fault. You can blame her, she doesn't mind. I hope you enjoy reading my fourth book which is about life from the perspective of my rather nutty collie dog, Flynn Jenkins.

Gertsje, Ann Greenwood's horse

Chapter 1
"We've Only Just Begun"

My name is Flynn Jenkins. I'm a Border collie with lots of energy and bags of personality. I am very busy and important and happen to be living my best life in Newquay Cornwall surrounded by friends and love and adventure. I'm pretty lucky really and, if you will listen, I will tell you my story.

I was born in a barn in October 2019. My mother is a working collie called Lady. I never met my father but I understand he is also is a working dog. I am one of five boys and I like to think I am the most attractive. I was the first to be picked out for a new home so I take that as a kind of confirmation of being the best of the bunch. My two brown blusher-like markings on both my cheeks make me look pretty and I consider they have some responsibility for my dashingly good looks and "must cuddle" appeal. My character is (reasonably) bold, affectionate, intelligent (although that is questioned sometimes), energetic, loyal, friendly and pretty smiley. My existence for the first twelve weeks of my life was in a straw-filled barn. Play, food, warmth, comfort and love with my siblings and mum for company. It was pretty noisy and manic but they were good times.

From the age of about eight weeks old a bedraggled looking lady attended the barn on a weekly basis. I liked her and we (all my siblings and I) would run over to her and give her lots of nudges and affection through the gaps of the bars of the gate that contained us in our barn home. She was to become my human mummy and actually that was fine by me. It was clear that she had lots of love to give.

Four weeks later, on Christmas Eve morning at 8am, she came along and scooped me up out of the chaos. I was transferred into the front seat of her 4x4 vehicle with her and I thanked her for her attention and choice by snuggling into her neck as hard as I could and clinging to her with my two front legs. She was going to love me with all her heart; I could feel it. I felt lucky and so happy. I had no idea what was around the corner in life. It was going to be different for sure I knew that and I was ready to embrace whatever it was.

Flynn and his brothers (he is second from the left)

Chapter 2
"Monster"

The car environment was comforting. I felt safe and as we set off the purr of the engine sent me dozing. I dreamt of being with my brothers in our barn. Flinging ourselves at each other, running, jumping, chewing, bouncing, and generally playing whilst Lady (our mummy) watched over us protectively ready to bark and snap at the heels of anyone who would disturb our safe haven.

After about ten minutes the engine came to a stop. I woke abruptly and I was lifted and lowered into what felt like a deep smelly swamp. It was cold, it was yuk. It was definitely not what I was used to or wanted. I was up to my elbows in thick cold mud. I felt a bit disgusted. Where was the straw and hay that I was so used to surrounding me?

Before I could further contemplate the unpleasant ground surface, huge scary sounds ensued. Breathing, snorting, stamping, squawking. It was obvious that my new human carer and I were not alone in this new unsavoury venue.

The strange noises from unknown frightening sources were all around. I could sense that the beings that surrounded us were far bigger than me and their physical form was something frighteningly unfamiliar. What they were I didn't know. All I could be sure of was that they were living, breathing creatures and I felt quite petrified.

I almost felt like I couldn't breathe or see anything. I was frozen in terror. I wanted to run but I couldn't. Where would I run anyway? I had no idea where I was. Where was my warm barn? Where were my brothers? Where was my mother? She'd protect me surely, but she and they were not there and they weren't coming to my rescue anytime soon. All I could do was cower and shiver in terror. What was this terrible place and why had I been brought here?

Chapter 3
"Turn the World On"

I continued to cower and shiver in nervousness and terror and was scooped up fairly quickly and carried by my human mummy further into the abyss. My frightened state was obvious to her and she lifted me kindly into a shed and placed me on top of some bins whilst feeds were made up for the noisy beasts.

As meals were busily prepared for the creatures a handful of dog biscuits was placed in front of me which I crunched through. I felt I needed fuel to survive this new episode so consumed my small ration quickly and gratefully. The feeds for the other creatures were then distributed.

I was then taken carefully out of the shed and carried into what I came to know as the yard. A concrete area surrounded by what looked like five individual small sheds with solid half doors. It was only then that I could properly take in the unusual beings that were around me.

Walking towards the feed shed at the end of the yard were two large, fat, fairly bald pink creatures. They were short and stout with big snouts and both regularly addressed by my human Mummy as "bad pig".

In addition, there was a spindly, relatively small (although still bigger than me) brown long-haired being with impressive horns who Mum called Heidi. Apparently, she was a goat. She really didn't like me. Her back stood up on end when she came close to me and she grew and pointed herself and her large horns at me as if to warn me off then she ran away. I felt she didn't mean it though. I felt fear from her. I think she'd been hurt or frightened by someone or something in the past and I somehow reminded her of that experience.

There were four white creatures with stringy necks and orange beaks who hissed, squawked, and ran fiercely towards me and Mum. I came to understand these were geese. Blue-eyed, beautiful, but loud and aggressive white birds. I wasn't sure whether they had names; the way Mum addressed them was generally with discontent and in a defensive tone. It didn't feel amicable on either part actually, which I think was instigated by their attitude rather than Mum's.

There were also five other animals who were far bigger than me. They peered over the small shed half doors that surrounded the yard. Long-faced, long-necked, long-legged, long-backed heavy-footed beasts apparently called horses. They all had names and different tones that they were spoken to by Mum but I couldn't keep up with it all. I was in awe of how big powerful and intimidating they were.

Finally, there were three females of the human kind, Mum and two others. All three of them in turn during my first morning at the yard gave me kisses and cuddles which I was grateful of given the intimidating surroundings.

I was far from at ease with the non-human creatures at the yard but decided that they needed the benefit of the doubt, and I had a deep-down feeling that most of them actually didn't want to kill me. I hoped I was right but, ultimately, time would tell. The humans at the yard at least were loving gentle and protective towards me, and I felt excited but quietly apprehensive about my new life and what was ahead for me.

The geese

Chapter 4
"Something Good Can Work"

We left the yard at lunchtime and continued on to a new destination. This was to be my new home. A terraced house in the centre of Newquay. A habitat of generous Victorian proportions arranged modestly over three floors. My area within this abode appeared to be in the kitchen. I had a material enclosure in that room which is where I was put to begin with when we arrived. It enabled me to take in my surroundings and my new company.

There were four other humans at this location. All different. Craig, an adult; firm, forgetful, loyal, and loving. The remaining three were much younger versions; they were children I believe. Aaron aged fifteen; kind and a little dopey. Emily aged fourteen; attentive and helpful. Kayan aged thirteen; quite loud, but sensitive and caring.

There were five felines; Smokey, Phoenix, Orlando, Mr Soft and Mr Burns. They were flighty chaseable creatures, and I felt a huge urge to get closer to them and get to know them better. They didn't seem to feel the same. Their overriding attitude was hostility towards me. In the room next to the kitchen lived two other beings; they were dogs, two bitches called Lexi and Bella.

The home environment was chaotic and circus-like. I felt a part of something however crazy and out of control that might be. I had a challenge ahead of me to be accepted and fit into this new life. I was going to try my hardest to oblige.

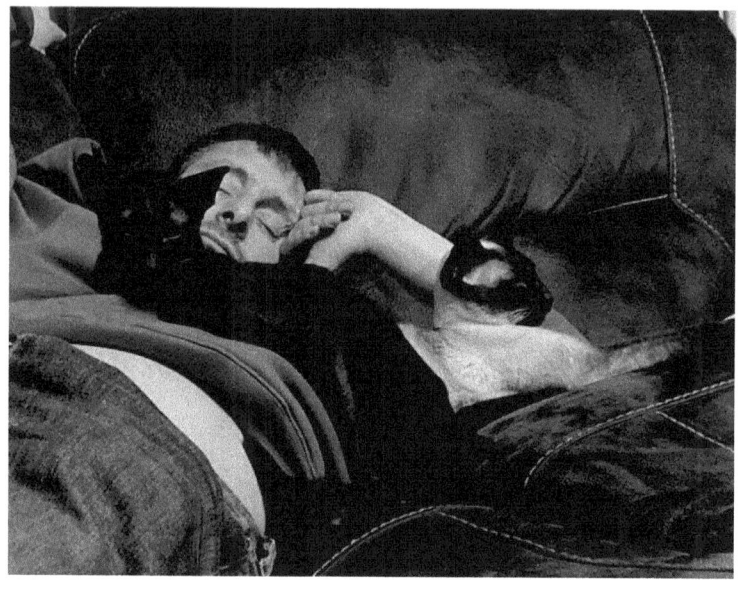

Craig with Orlando and Phoenix

Chapter 5
"What a Difference a Day Makes"

The next sunrise I was up early and had a walk with the two other dogs who weren't sure of me by any stretch of the imagination. I was then whisked off in the car to the yard. I was cradled for most of the time by Mum. The times she couldn't carry me I was put into the living quarters of the horses. These were apparently called stables and were full of straw which I found quite comforting.

One of the horses was called Diva. She was loving, gentle, and fascinated by me. She was so affectionate but I was wary of her attention. She was literally a hundred times bigger than me, as were the other four horses, but out of all of them she loved me the most and was careful and cautious around me. She shared her breakfast with me.

Buddy, who lived next door to Diva, was older, wiser, and less forgiving. He was a little clumsy or thoughtless or both and managed to stand on me. He released the physical pressure on me as soon as Mum asked him to. I cried, I really cried. It hurts when horses stand on you. I was comforted for a long time by Mum whilst Buddy, with the whites of his eyes showing, worriedly looked on wondering what it was that he had done wrong and what all the noise was about.

Gertsje, another of the horses, made lots of angry faces at me over her door, but I didn't feel like she meant it. She didn't want to hurt me, I felt that. Danny, the only pony, made horrid faces that would escalate to attacks. I was very frightened of him and thankfully wasn't left in his company for very long.

My most favourite of the horse herd was Corgan. He was interested in me but not obsessed. He allowed me in his space and was gently inquisitive towards me; he just sniffed and was quietly investigative. There was no aggression at all from him. Just curiosity. I spent lots of time in his stable.

Heidi and the four geese decided to keep their distance from me. If they considered I got too close to them they would show their objection by way of increased noise or making themselves look bigger. The whole environment was interesting, exciting and, much less frightening than it had been the previous day.

Picture of Flynn and Diva

Chapter 6
"Better Days"

My relationships with the animals at the yard have come to involve work, compromise and negotiation. It takes a fair amount of effort for me to try and get everyone to behave appropriately. Not all are obedient or compliant and one in particular I do not attempt to discipline much because she is near perfect. I do think I have the measure of all of the yard animals pretty well though.

Turns out the two large bald pink creatures are pigs with individual names: Thelma and Louise. I have more suitable names for both of them. Thelma should be called Grumpy because she grumbles a lot and Louise should be called Chatty as she always has something to say. She's particularly chatty when eating her food.

Mum tells me that they both used to live next door in a concrete shed and that she looked after them from time to time when the owner went away on holiday. She heard that the owner planned to sell them to go to slaughter for sausage meat so stepped in and bought them both in an effort to save their lives. They moved to the yard a few years ago and have since lived a happy free-range life.

They don't do much. They get up to eat their breakfast (which they generally fight over even though they get exactly the same portion in two separate bowls) and then, after a bit of foraging in the field, lie down and sleep until dinner time. After dinner (which sometimes involves another food-related brawl) they go to back to their pig house together, cuddle up and go to sleep.

They don't bother me really and I'm no longer scared of them. They do try and get into the feed shed now and then and when they do they collectively get called "bad pig". I assist in these moments by nipping on both their heels to aid in moving them away from said forbidden feed shed.

Heidi and the geese are an interesting bunch. Heidi has an obsession with the geese and I have heard Mum say that she thinks maybe Heidi mistakenly thinks that she is actually a goose as she follows them everywhere and goes to bed with them in the caravan every evening. The geese, however, are not particularly friendly. Their names are Rod, Jane, Freddie and Hissy. Freddie is Hissy's father and those two boys are the most unpleasant of the four. They charge, peck and hiss very aggressively almost simultaneously. They are nicknamed "The Krays" because they are vicious and horrid to everyone including Heidi. She, however, remains dedicated to them like a loyal battered housewife.

I am able to move the geese around by running at them, but it's not aesthetically pleasing or very satisfying. It's quite messy. They tend to scatter in chaos rather than neatly move the way I have suggested. It also most of the time results in them turning on me. Sometimes, however, they will just aggressively attack me for no reason at all and just because they feel like it. I've had a few bites from them. They have quite sharp teeth and a surprisingly strong crocodile-like grip. Mum has had to intervene a few times to get them to let go of me. She shouts and runs at them and they eventually reluctantly release me. I never ever hurt them even when they are hurting me.

Mum has told me several times what a good boy I am after she has prised them off me. On those occasions she whispers to me that she wouldn't have blamed me if I'd decided to have a bit of a chomp back in self-defence. I won't though. It's not in my nature.

The Krays even stupidly have a go at the horses now and then. They are proper bird brains. This doesn't generally go down very well. Hissy has had a couple of unplanned flying lessons as a consequence. He's received a swift kick from his chosen horse victim rendering him quickly but briefly airborne. Miraculously he has come away unscathed and it's not put him off planning and executing further attacks.

Heidi is quite lovely. She's a bit timid but very sweet. Mum said no one could get anywhere near Heidi when she first came to the yard. She didn't want to be touched and would run away from everyone except the geese. She however has become much braver and more relaxed over time.

When she is hungry she goes into the feed shed and headbutts the feed bin until someone gets her some food. She also quite often lies in amongst the horse's hay and although she will never be cuddly, she will tolerate being touched now. In the mornings she runs down the yard to greet the human workers at the gate to see what food treats they may have brought her. She loves bread (as long as it's white) and ginger nuts and will let the humans hand-feed her.

Although she was unsure about me when I first arrived, she has since taken quite an interest and we are great friends. I rarely herd her. I don't feel she needs or deserves it.

As soon as I got a bit bigger, we started to play matador-like games together. This involves me growling and playfully running away and dodging her whilst she charges at me, trying to butt me with her impressive horns. She does manage to pin me a few times during these games but most of the time I am too quick for her. On the few occasions she does win she is very gentle in her victory and always quickly releases me after smirking triumphantly. It is great fun. Heidi is my best animal friend. Playing with her at the yard is my most favourite thing.

Thelma and Louise (with Emily)

Chapter 7
"The Hype"

As the months passed, I also started to get to know my animal friends at home a lot better mainly through intense observation and attentive listening. The cats are really quite fascinating to me. Smokey belongs to Craig. He is named according to his colour. He's a Turkish Angora cross. Mum doesn't really like him. She says he's a suck up to Craig (who adores him) and that deep down he's a bully, particularly to Orlando and Phoenix for no reason whatsoever. I would agree with her. I've seen it with my own eyes. Smokey is the most intriguing of all the cats for me. Ninety percent of my attention whilst in the house is dedicated to escort and herding services for him alone. In my honest opinion he needs to be accompanied in most of his travels, particularly around the kitchen area.

Smokey and I have lots of conversations and interactions together. He thanks me for the personal service I provide to him by way of remodelling my nose with various scratches together with a personal song of gratitude which consists of hissing and growling. His song is loudest in the morning at breakfast time when my level of attention and duty is at absolute maximum. Together we participate in what Mum describes as a cat and dog version of the Argentine tango. I may be wrong but I get the impression by his tone and demeanour that he is not overly keen on me as his dancing partner but he needs to appreciate that I am merely carrying out my necessary duties. He should actually be impressed by my efficiency, dedication and commitment to service.

Phoenix and Orlando are Siamese brothers. Phoenix is chocolate and Orlando is seal point. They ask very loudly for food at set times of the day and Mum always obliges. Phoenix is Mum's cat. In the evenings when she is sat down in the front room you can always find him curled up on her lap. He was really unwell a few years ago with a suspected tumour on the lung, and despite professionals advising Mum that the kindest thing would be to put him to sleep, she managed to nurse him back to full health with love, food and the help of natural remedies. For this reason, he adores her and waits loyally for her at the front door when she is out. When she is at home he follows her around the house, everywhere. Orlando is very affectionate and beautiful but pretty fickle. He will cuddle up to and love anyone who is available, even if he's never met them before.

Mr Burns and Mr Soft are almost identical brothers. They are black Siamese cross Burmese. Mr Soft is called so as he is incredibly soft to touch. I would agree with that. The times I have herded him and my teeth have gently caressed his ankles I have thought to myself how soft and lovely he feels in my mouth. He has a constant fairly vacant look on his face. He is extremely bright and wide-eyed and his expression is one of constant surprise and shock. Rabbit caught in headlights comes to mind. Despite the bright look on his face, he has what I would describe as a meagre offering of brain cells. The lights are on and almost blinding but there's barely anyone at home. His focus is pretty much just food and sleep. He can mainly be found in the window watching and squeaking at birds (potential food) or sleeping on Mum's bed cuddled up with his brother Mr Burns.

Mr Burns is called so as he reminded Mum (who named him) of a character from a television series called *The Simpsons* when he first came to the Jenkins' house. He was apparently rather tiny but "adorable". I can't imagine how he was ever tiny. He's rather a fat lump in my eyes, perhaps still adorable though. Mr Burns is also quite wide-eyed but it's not as exaggerated as Mr Soft. I think he was blessed with slightly more brain cells than his brother. He is very much a lap cat and loves cuddles, kisses and general interaction. Sleep is his most favourite thing. Mr Soft, Mr Burns, Phoenix and Orlando also require fairly regular herding from me but not to extent of Smokey. That will likely never change. They are all fairly compliant and accepting of the service I provide to them in this regard, unlike Smokey.

The two other dogs of the household quite like me. We are now good friends and walk and run together regularly on the beach. Bella is a black Patterdale cross Springer Spaniel. She is scatty, enthusiastic and energetic, although not as energetic as me. She does however give me a good run around when we go for walks on the beach together where I practise my herding skills on her. According to her she holidayed in Kidderminster for a couple of months by herself over a decade ago and was the subject of a nationwide search on book Face (whatever that is) where thousands tried to FindBella. Sounds a bit farfetched to me but she's adamant it's true.

Lexi is a golden Rhodesian Ridgeback cross. She's a lot slower than Bella and me when it comes to running, and is the eldest of the three of us. She is a big softy but a real loud mouth when someone comes to the front door. Bella and I now join in with barking when someone knocks on the front door. It doesn't go down very well with the humans but it's great fun and a good opportunity to have a regular good old sing song together.

There's also talk in the house on occasion of a cat called Fudge Jenkins. His lifetime was before mine but everyone regards him as a bit of a legend. He had lots of adventures and a great personality. Apparently, he was the "best pet ever". We shall see about that.

Smokey and Flynn doing the Argentine Tango

Chapter 8
"Live More and Love More"

The largest of the yard animals are the horses. All with very different personalities and a varying tolerance for me and my established and dedicated work ethic. I'd seen cows before at the farm I was born in but horses are arguably bigger and much more interesting in my opinion.

Gertsje is a black Friesian mare. She is not the biggest of the horses at the yard, but she certainly carries her head the highest which makes her look huge. She's a horse whose presence takes your breath away, she doesn't have to do anything to shine. She's effortlessly beautiful.

She has a fantastic array of facial expressions at her disposal which she displays at varying times depending on her mood. She can look both utterly beautiful and absolutely terrifying. Her terrifying look is achieved by pinning her ears flat to her head making her resemble a kind of fire-breathing dragon.

Gertsje directs her best frightening faces at me when I'm busy working outside her stable door. She finds me working hard close to her quite irritating it would seem. I think a busy environment causes her quite a bit of stress. Her answer to feeling threatened is to make herself very big, pull terrible faces, snort very loudly to let everyone know that she is on high alert and then attempt to run away from whatever it is that she is convinced is out to kill her.

She isn't actually terrifying or fierce deep down. She is soft and sweet with a fair amount of insecurity and anxiety mixed in. She has never tried to hurt me she just makes lots of faces to suggest that she might. I've yet to feel she means it. She's fairly obedient when I assist in herding her out of her stable and into the field although the terrible faces do appear as a slight objection.

Corgan is really nice to me. He has been since the day I arrived at the yard. He is a God in my eyes. In fact, he should be called King or Prince Corgan. He is dark bay and damn handsome with it, and he knows it. He is without a doubt awe-inspiring to me. He can move any one of the other animals at the yard just by looking at them a certain way or moving his ears. If anyone dare to miss these first two cues from him he is quick to move his body towards them menacingly, and they quickly oblige. His level of importance, respect and power is something else.

I will have to ask him for some tips as although I have a fair amount of success with my herding skills, I physically have to work really hard at it. Corgan does barely anything and the animals part like the Red Sea.

His personality from what I can see is demanding, obnoxious and a little arrogant but nonetheless everyone loves him. Mum says he is actually her favourite horse. He makes his demands known by banging on his stable door. He bangs when he wants food, he bangs when he wants attention, he bangs when he wants to go out. His needs are generally met as and when he demands. He saunters around the yard and the field like he owns the place and he pretty much does. He is in charge particularly when it comes to the other animals. He does sometimes forget himself and tries to intimidate the humans too but he is soon reminded kindly that that isn't acceptable behaviour simply by being told "no." He then quietly goes back to bossing the animals around instead. I don't tend to herd him too much because he kicks out at me in objection.

Buddy is funny. He is elderly, cheeky, grumpy at times and a bit clumsy. (Remember he stood on me the first day I came to the yard.) He appears to have several nicknames. Buddy Grump and Muddy Buddy are the most frequently used. He is the most spoilt horse on the yard. He makes cute small whickering noises so that treats are supplied to him almost constantly by the humans. He has beautiful soft eyes and is very loveable. According to Mum he is one in a million.

Buddy has an unhealthy obsession with the muck heap which he makes a beeline for most days. He likes to roll around on it but manages to get himself into positions where he is unable to get back up on his feet without assistance so we don't let him visit it. I help ensure that he does not go anywhere near it with my herding skills.

Diva is a very beautiful bay mare. She apparently was very fragile mentally and physically when she first arrived at the yard a few years ago but, according to Mum, has really come out of her shell and developed a lovely happy personality over the years. She is sweet, soft, forgiving, loving and quite maternal (particularly towards me). She is always eating and for that reason Mum has given her the nickname of Miss Piggy. She is the easiest of the horses for me to move around. A small amount of pressure from me results in pretty fast forward movement from her and sometimes some acrobatics. She can be pretty energetic.

Danny is my least favourite of the five horses. He is actually a pony rather than a horse which from what I can ascertain is just a slightly smaller version of a horse. He is black and white which Mum says is officially described as piebald. He can be quite pushy, reactive and jumpy. I think he finds it hard to relax. He doesn't seem to like me much and to be honest the feeling is kind of mutual. He too makes faces over his stable door at me but it's different to Gertsje. I can feel he really means it. He tries to bite and stamp on me and has been known to chase me in the field with hatred in his eyes. I tend to not assist too much in moving him around. Call it self-preservation.

There is a puzzling activity that he and the humans do together. He wears a headcollar with a rope and a chosen human holds the end of the rope with either one or two hands. He then proceeds suddenly at quite a pace to a set destination (normally across the field) with said human trailing behind him also at some speed. It's quite curious to watch. I'm not sure whether it's a consensual activity.

Generally whichever human is at the end of the rope seems to be struggling to keep up and eventually has to let go after demonstrating what can only be described as a period of mud or grass skiing (depending on the time of year) whilst calling his name multiple times in a panicked manner. Maybe it's supposed to be a race? In which case, Danny always wins.

Picture of Corgan (on left) and Danny (on right)

Chapter 9
"We Don't Talk Anymore"

The months trickled on and I settled into a very happy routine split mostly between the yard and home. There were times when Mum and Craig would take me for walks around Newquay which sometimes involved going to the pub where she and Craig would meet friends and chat for a few hours. I liked accompanying them on these visits. These were social times rather than work and, as a young handsome dog, lots of people would come and say hello and give me cuddles and attention which I really enjoyed.

This sadly didn't last as talk of a pandemic swooped in followed by "lockdown". I wasn't really sure what any of this meant but for me it seemed that the mood of the collective was low, guarded and a bit frightened. People stopped saying hello and nobody was really allowed to leave the house unless it was essential.

Aaron, Emily and Kayan remained at home rather than going to school every day which meant I got to spend more time with them. Mum and I still got to go to the yard though as looking after the animals was obviously essential. I missed the social butterflying during this uncertain period but enjoyed the close time with family it brought.

During this time Lexi collapsed. Mum wanted the vet to come to her at home as Lexi couldn't seem to move her legs but, due to lockdown, this wasn't a possibility. She was gently lifted into the car and Mum and Craig drove her to the vets. The diagnosis wasn't good. She had suspected heart failure and didn't make it back home. This was my first experience of loss, and, although I had only had Lexi in my life for less than a year, I loved her and considered her family. I missed her, as did everyone.

It was very quiet in the house without her. She had always instigated the chorus that followed any knock at the front door. Out of respect and grief Bella and I didn't sing our doggy doorbell song for a while. We would resume it again one day, in Lexi's memory, but exactly when would depend on when Bella was ready. The whole family was sad when we lost Lexi but, Bella was the saddest. Lexi had been her best friend and companion for ten years.

Mum felt sorry for Bella and so allowed her to come with us to the yard for a few days. Bella was very happy at the yard and ran around a lot. As usual, I practised my herding skills on her. It was great fun. However, on the third day, suddenly, whilst we were running in the field, her hunting instinct kicked in and she locked onto the geese and immediately pursued them at lightning speed with deadly intent. Mum desperately screamed Bella's name at the top of her voice over and over again as she watched on in terror. With every ounce of her being. Mum willed Bella to stop, listen and come to call but, Bella was so focused on her prey, she didn't or couldn't hear her.

Bella managed to separate the birds into pairs and two of them flew towards the stream with her in hot pursuit. As Bella plunged herself into the stream there was a large splash, a scattering of feathers and then, an eery silence. At this moment she seemed to regain her ability to hear and, as Mum called her name for what seemed like the hundredth time, Bella actually responded and sulked back to the yard with her tail between her legs, realising the error of her ways. Mum gave her a strong verbal scolding, confined her in a stable and went to inspect the crime scene. I accompanied her.

We were both expecting to find at least one goose carcass as a result of the incident. However, although there were a few feathers in the stream, there was no sign of the two of the geese that had headed there. They had disappeared. Freddie and his son Hissy had fled in fear leaving Rod and Jane behind. Mum and I spent some hours over the next couple of days searching for them in the surrounding fields to no avail.

Despite The Krays not being particularly friendly Mum was sad that they were gone and feared that not being safely put to bed in the caravan each evening would make them potential prey for the foxes that roam the area. For that reason, we were to keep looking and put the word out to the neighbours to keep an eye out for them. Understandably, Bella isn't allowed to come to the yard anymore as she can't be trusted around the geese.

The seasons changed again and we were faced with another winter. Winter is wet, cold and muddy at the yard. I get covered in mud everyday which means before we head home I get a bath which I'm not too keen on. Mum has to lead me to the hose and wash me down. I reluctantly stand to get washed. The towel drying afterwards, however, is a nice experience.

There is apparently another lockdown around the corner. I'm sure we will all manage to get through it. Bella and I will look forward to celebrating the end of lockdown with doggy doorbell songs.

Lexi

Chapter 10
"Dream Job"

As well as an eclectic collection of animals at the yard, there is human company too, other than Mum. They all come to help look after the animals that live there. There have been several faces come and go at the yard since I arrived. As my time at the yard is very busy I haven't really bothered to get to know all of them, especially those who have come and then for whatever reason left. I've been too busy working to make friends really. There's lots of work to do and it's always been my priority to get that work done as quickly and efficiently as possible. Making new friends has been, and is, a low priority.

In addition to Mum, however, five female humans have stayed for the long haul. They have, like me, remained committed, loyal and enthusiastic (but not as enthusiastic as me) in their efforts to keep the animals well cared for. I have therefore come to call these ladies my friends.

Cheryl is the most long-standing worker. She was at the yard the day I arrived and I know her the best. Loyal, funny, hardworking and caring. She is soft and affectionate towards me.

Moyà is the oldest of the humans at the yard. Mum says she's older than Buddy which is quite a feat as I know Buddy is really old. She works pretty hard despite her considerable age. She's very chatty and kind, especially to

Buddy and me, and brings a bag of snacks to the yard when she comes which are not all meant for me. She does also bring me a dog biscuit, but I choose my moment when to eat it. If I'm busy working it has to wait until later.

April and her daughter Brooke also come and help. April is confident, knowledgeable and helpful. Her daughter Brooke is quiet but works hard and cares deeply about all the animals.

Julie is another hard worker. She is very talkative but her voice sounds very different to everyone else. Mum says she is Welsh. When she first started coming to the yard Mum had to keep asking Julie to repeat herself as she couldn't understand what she was saying but she seems to have got the hang of it now. Julie likes cuddling Diva when no one is looking. I think she really loves her.

By the time I was eighteen months old I was managing the work at the yard with the help of my human female friends extremely efficiently. We all had our roles, and we adhered and executed our tasks expertly. As well as working, I supervised everything and I was generally pleased with the standard of workmanship everyone delivered. Moyà affectionately calls the yard Paradise Club as we (humans and animals) are all so happy there. Despite everyone being there predominately to work, it is a lovely place to be.

At this time unknown to us all, something ominous was looming at Paradise Club. An uninvited and unwelcome resident was hiding in the background, and for a while remained unnoticed. It's numbers were to shortly rapidly increase and it was going to get out of hand, causing worry, concern and a major issue. Some drastic action was going to be necessary to deal with it, and very soon.

Mum, Corgan, April, Gertsje, Diva and Brooke

Chapter 11
"Lose Control"

Let me just start by saying Mum loves animals. She wouldn't want to intentionally hurt any animal. She, as a young girl, used to spend time rescuing flies out of the horses' water buckets to stop them from drowning. Yes, I know, flies are insects not animals but I'm trying to make a point.

When she was thirteen years old, she tried to help a fox that had unwisely ventured into a ditch filled with frozen water. The fox ended up biting her when she outstretched her hand in an offer of help. She has a scar on one of her fingers on her left hand as a reminder of her act of "stupid" kindness. She also told me that when she was seventeen years old, she braked so hard whilst driving to avoid hitting a rabbit one time that she managed to spin the car 180 degrees. She avoided the rabbit though and luckily didn't hurt herself or damage the car in the process. So, to recap, Mum loves animals. She cares about them, tries to help them and wouldn't want to ever hurt or cause suffering to them. Hold that thought for a moment.

Heidi and her goose friends had now been living at the yard for just over two years, and the pigs a little more than that. Feeding these animals quite often involved food scraps being thrown on the ground for them to consume. I think this may have played a part in us having a few more creatures of a particular type move into the yard uninvited. They were, of course, rats.

To begin with, Mum thought they were cute. She found three baby rats running around in the bottom of an empty feed bin one morning and naively and kindly released them. They then must have scurried back to all their relatives and announced to the collective that the feed shed was the place to go and eat and that there was no consequence or danger there.

What happened in the following weeks verged on carnage and it was not cute in any way, shape or form. The population of rats seemed to explode to the point that plastic feed bins were being chewed through and horses' rugs that were in storage in the feed shed were shredded.

Mum tried her best to find an animal-loving solution to the growing issue. The thought of the alternative was unbearable. She bought metal feed bins, barricaded the shed door firmly shut and fed the geese and pigs using buckets. Any food that wasn't consumed in one sitting was secured in locked metal bins. She thought that would be enough to deter the rats and that, without readily available food, they would move on and find somewhere else to live. It wasn't enough though. They didn't move on and it got even worse. Very soon we had a really BIG rat problem.

Let me just clarify. There wasn't ONE really big rat; there were what felt like HUNDREDS of them. Rats were everywhere, all the time. Even in the daytime. In broad daylight you would see them running around. Some of them were quite brazen and would wander through the yard almost casually. I heard a visiting friend say to Mum one day, "If you see the rats in the day then you have a really big issue as they only normally come out at night. There must be loads of them."

Feed time for the horses became a bit of a nightmare. Buddy has a large feed for two reasons, one, he is a little spoilt, and two, because he needs it. He is elderly and doesn't have many teeth left so is a slow eater with a large feed to consume.

When his food bowl was placed on the floor a frenzied excited rat party would ensue. Think rats leaving a sinking ship, except they are not leaving, they are swarming around Buddy's feet whilst screeching almost like vultures eyeing up their prey. The high-pitched screeching and visual made it look like something out of a horror movie. The objective was clearly to be an eating competition. If Mum had allowed it, the rats would no doubt have eaten most, if not all, of Buddy's food.

Initially Mum had to hold Buddy's feed bowl for him whilst he ate. She ended up buying a feed bowl that hung on the stable door to enable him to eat his food whilst screeching and scurrying chaos carried on underneath him. Some drastic action had to be taken. Mum hated the idea, but it was necessary however uncomfortable.

Mum holding Buddy's feed for him

Chapter 12
"Worth It"

Ratman was a shrivelled scrawny weed of a man. Thin, short and quite drawn. I decided he was probably older than he looked. Physically he looked like he had had a hard long life. I would presume he spent his life smoking more cigarettes, than eating hot dinners. Appropriately there would always be half a lit rollie hanging out of his mouth when he arrived at the yard. As soon as he finished that one, he would be rolling another to replace it.

His job was to get rid of the rats and this was to be achieved by putting down traps filled with poison. Mum was very uncomfortable about this. I heard her have the same conversation with him several times, reiterating that she really didn't want to kill the rats but that she had reluctantly come to the conclusion that their presence was overpowering and could not continue. She also reminded him multiple times that the traps had to be 100 percent secure so that there was no chance of pigs, geese, or me, getting into them and getting hold of any poison.

When he had first arrived, he had spotted several rats running under and around the caravan that Heidi and the geese slept in overnight. Such was his passion for extermination of rats that this almost enraged him. "I'll get those nasties don't you worry. I'll get them!" He placed a couple of traps around the yard and a few under the caravan.

Ratman came regularly to check progress and restock the traps as necessary. On one of his many visits, he was inspecting the area under the caravan. As well as sleeping in there overnight, Heidi would also sometimes go in there during the day to rest. It could be quite a suntrap, especially where she sat. She adopted one of the caravan seats near the door and it came to be known as "Heidi's throne". On this particular day, Heidi happened to be sat on her throne.

Whilst Ratman was busy bending down looking under the caravan for "nasty" rats, Heidi took offence. She rose from her throne and butted Ratman on the bottom causing him to spit out his treasured rollie and almost fall over. He was quite taken aback, but once recovered he proceeded to have a very short wrestling match with Heidi.

Holding on to both her horns he tried to prise her out of the caravan, but due to his weedy frame and lack of muscle, he was unsuccessful. Mutterings continued from him for a few minutes whilst the pathetic struggle carried on. He eventually relented, let go of her horns and stormed off back to his car to roll another cigarette and head home. Heidi victoriously returned to her throne and got back to sunbathing without the irritating sunblock that had so rudely interrupted her session.

Ratman came almost every day for a few months and was quite successful in getting the rat population under control. I heard from Mum, however, that it was quite expensive getting him to constantly manage the situation. Surely there had to be a more cost-effective form of long-term pest control? Mum said she would have to give it some thought.

Heidi sitting on her throne

Chapter 13
"All This Love"

Another winter came upon us (my second) and a new horse friend joined the yard. Her name, rather appropriately, was Pretty. She is a piebald like Danny but much bigger and, obviously, very beautiful. Affectionate, attention-seeking and impatient. Always pleased to see the humans, and although she is pushy, a bit snappy and stubborn, she is loveable and can be very sweet. Mum has a real soft spot for her. I catch Mum in Pretty's stable sometimes kissing Pretty on the muzzle over and over again. Pretty shows softness in her eyes during these moments, absolutely lapping up the attention.

Pretty has mixed emotions about me. Similar faces over the stable door to Gertsje and Danny with a varying level of animosity. Sometimes she isn't too bothered when I am busy working outside her door, other times she really can't stand it. She is very playful in the field and there are days where she encourages me to join in but other times when I am definitely not invited and she is very fast and determined in seeing me off. Corgan always instigates the playtimes (of course he does) but she is more than willing to participate.

Mum was still pondering what best to do to keep the rat population under control long-term and came up with rather a brilliant idea. She said if we got a yard cat they would hopefully manage it for us and it would be far more economical than employing Ratman on a permanent basis. Great. I love cats.

The hunt for a suitable feline began. It didn't take long to find one. A feral kitten was offered to Mum by a lady from a local rescue. She was called Nancy and was in need of a new home. Although Mum thought an adult cat would have been more suitable she agreed to take her on.

When she arrived, Nancy was beyond timid and frightened. The advice was to have her contained in a dog cage for a couple of weeks in a secure area to help her adjust to her surroundings and settle in. A cage was stationed in the feed shed and that became her initial living quarters. Every time anyone went into the shed Nancy would hiss then quickly disappear under her cat bed. This seemed puzzling behaviour to me. Despite this strange behaviour Mum, Moyà and Cheryl made a point of chatting away to her whilst in the shed.

Mum, for the first week, would twice a day go into the feed shed for a few minutes and just gently talk to Nancy. No pressure, just conversation. I would stand outside peering through the wooden slats in the shed, listening, observing and (most importantly) guarding. Mum would sit on the floor in the middle of the shed and tell Nancy how beautiful and loved she was and how happy she was going to be living at the yard.

By the end of the first week Nancy became quite inquisitive and a little vocal. She started joining in conversation with occasional tiny meows. She stopped hiding so much and even wanted to be stroked a little. Just over two weeks and she was to be released out of the cage but still contained in the shed. Spending a week loose in the feed shed did her the world of good and her confidence grew even more. She got to the point of not hiding when people opened the shed door and actually approaching and greeting Mum with lovely leg rubs at meal times.

Four weeks after she arrived, she was finally given full freedom and despite Mum being very worried about letting her out and leaving her overnight, she was happily waiting for us both in the morning under the shed. She was a little nervous of me to begin with but now she strolls quite happily around me. She doesn't require any herding. Unlike the cats at home, she is extremely well behaved.

Mum hoped hunting would follow soon, but we were all a little concerned whether she would even be able to catch anything as Nancy was so small. We needn't have worried though. Although it took some time, she did become, and remains, a great hunter.

Nancy has developed such a sassy and funny personality now. She is very vocal and has become incredibly friendly, but can be moody, bossy and demanding. She comes for her food twice a day every day. If it is not prepared promptly enough she will grumble and gently smack or bite whichever human is in the feed shed to remind them that the priority should be preparing her meal right NOW. She likes to accompany Mum and me when we poo pick the field, all the while rubbing our legs and singing a happy catty song. She loves hunting but also enjoys a sleep either on top of haynets hung up in the stables or snuggled into the hay or straw bales in the yard. She gets spoilt by Moyà who brings her special cat biscuits which she savours and enjoys. Despite her great hunting skills, she isn't the best ratter. That became apparent fairly quickly. She is a fairly small cat and some rats are probably almost as big as her. Nancy, therefore, couldn't be the only yard cat. We were going to need backup at some point.

Pretty

Nancy

Chapter 14
"Paradise"

Six months had passed since Bella had chased two of the geese, Hissy and Freddie, into disappearance. Mum received a phone call late afternoon one day from a neighbour and friend who had spotted both geese less than two miles away whilst out riding her horse. It seemed quite miraculous that it was even possible that they were both still alive. A whole winter of not being fed and having no shelter or protection overnight meant we had all assumed they had perished or been eaten by Mr Fox. Obviously not. They are clearly hardy, strong birds to have survived on their own.

A brief rescue mission by Mum, Cheryl and Emily ensued involving some rugby-like tackling to catch both of them. They were brought home safely where there was a very noisy but happy goose reunion. Heidi's face when they returned was an absolute picture. She had got used to there being just two instead of four geese and seemed very confused that there were now double the amount of geese in front of her. She did a double take over and over again as if she couldn't believe her eyes. The extreme confusion on her face was entertaining. It was a very genuine "What the …….?" moment.

It had been pretty peaceful with just Rod and Jane at the yard. Now there were four geese again, the volume of noise increased dramatically.

For a moment Paradise Club was restored and complete again. Despite The Krays not being very nice, they were part of our clan and belonged at the yard with us all. Six months had passed, meaning that Hissy had come back to the yard at two years old. He was now mature. He and Freddie were also now very strongly bonded due to their private adventure. Rod and Jane, due to having just each other for those six months, were also bonded pretty firmly. It was mating season when The Krays returned to us. What could possibly go wrong?

Operation goose rescue

Chapter 15
"Bad Guy"

Aggressive became an understatement for describing the behaviour of the geese during mating season. The Krays were very quickly living up to their name and reputation again, but actually the behaviour of all three ganders became quite vicious. They would attack the pigs (Thelma and Louise), the humans and me without reason. I was regularly protected by Mum. They would also sometimes fight amongst themselves. Mum would regularly break up these fights. She called it "goose wrestling". From my perspective it involved her shouting, chasing and (if any of them turned on her) a kind of shot put-like throw with the offending goose flung away.

To add to this, Jane would be laying eggs and then nesting. This was also something that Mum had to deal with. Although she had two years prior allowed Jane to have two babies (of which Hissy was the only survivor) there were apparently to be no more geese added to the gaggle. This meant that Mum would have to remove any eggs that Jane chose to sit on. This was a challenge on more than one occasion but necessary.

The routine in the afternoon would often involve Craig driving Mum and me to the yard. Craig would then take me for a short walk down the road whilst Mum tended to putting the geese and horses to bed. One day on return to the yard after my walk with Craig, we both, as usual, got comfortable in the car and waited for Mum. I watched her walk down the yard and head to the caravan with a look of determination on her face. Unbeknown to her at the time, she was being very closely stalked by The Krays. As she stepped into the caravan The Krays rushed in after her. A commotion then followed.

The whole caravan proceeded to rock from side to side quite violently, like some sort of horror-filled fairground ride. We could hear squawking and shouting, and through the dirty windows we could just about make out the flapping of several pairs of wings. After a few seconds, Mum emerged out of the caravan quite red-faced carrying Jane and a couple of goose eggs. She was closely followed by three very angry-looking male geese. Mum fought off the boys as she released Jane and then walked over to the car and passed the goose eggs to Craig.

"What were you doing in the caravan?" asked Craig.
Mum's reply was, "I went to get Jane off her eggs. Rod was in there guarding her and, to add to the situation, The Krays followed me in. Obviously, none of them were very happy about me being there." It had clearly been a challenging goose-wrestling incident all whilst carrying a very upset goose and a couple of eggs. Well done Mum.

The geese and Heidi all went to bed in the caravan every night. They had done this from the first day they arrived at the yard. When The Krays came back home, the routine of putting all five of them to bed together each night soon became established again. Mating season had started though and their aggression was at an all-time high, so quite quickly Heidi decided that staying in the caravan with them overnight was no longer for her. I considered that a sensible decision.

One morning Mum and I arrived at the yard as usual and went (as we always did) to open the caravan and let the geese out. It was uncomfortably quiet as we approached. Normally there was considerable goose chat going on in the caravan as they spotted us through the windows walking towards them, but today it was deathly quiet. Something didn't feel right. As Mum flung the door open, Rod came running out at quite a speed and sprinted off into the field. Mum didn't seem to notice, but I could see that he was bumping into things as he ran. Mum left the other geese to trundle out leisurely and headed up to the feed shed to make up feeds.

Ten minutes passed and Rod was still running around with no set direction and in rather a frenzied manner. Mum stopped what she was doing and went to go and investigate. Getting near him was not difficult (which is not normally the case) and as she got closer the sight of him took her breath away.

Mum's geese all have strikingly blue eyes, but Rod's eyes were now pure white. He also looked quite battered. He was missing feathers on the top of his head, his neck and around both wings, and in places you could see his skin had been broken. Initially Mum thought he had lost both eyes, but on closer inspection his eyes were just covered with a white foam blocking his sight completely. She quickly worked out that he had had rather a severe beating from The Krays. Mum separated Rod and Jane from Hissy and Freddie and put her thinking cap on.

Once separated, with Jane as company, the foam that was blocking his sight dissipated from his eyes and he healed well over the next few days. The fighting was all about Jane. The boys were fighting over the only female goose available to them. This couldn't continue. The short-term fix was that whilst it was mating season they would have to go to bed separately. Rod and Jane together and Hissy and Freddie together. Mum could only think of one practical long-term solution. We were going to need more females.

Hissy attacking Flynn

Chapter 16
"Lost in Yesterday"

Mating season came and went and the geese calmed down a little bit. Mum managed to find some potential girlfriends for the boys and four female goslings came to the yard at the end of May. The feed was moved to another location in the yard and the feed shed became the home of the baby girls for the time being. They got a little outside supervised time every day where Mum followed them around like Mother Hen and hand-fed them grass. They were very cute and fascinating. Tiny compared to the adult geese; yellow, adorable balls of fluff.

After about two weeks of settling-in time, the goslings started to get a little vocal whilst having their outside time, and one day while Mum was supervising their daily walk, they started calling. Jane, who was the other side of the field, answered them and came running over. From that moment on she adopted them and looked after them like her own. She went to bed with them every night and they followed her around everywhere, fully accepting her as their mother goose.

The Krays and Rod watched over the girls intensely once Jane adopted them. They too were very accepting of the new arrangement. The three boys were put to bed in the caravan overnight for this time. They seemed quite happy with this and every morning picked up their guarding and supervision duties of Jane and her new babies.

Once fully grown (which happened surprisingly fast) Rod was put to bed with all the girls. He wanted to go in with them, and Jane seemed to need him. The Krays were left to guard the whole yard overnight, which was fine by them. They had, after all, spent a whole winter outdoors and managed perfectly well. Mum actually said it would be a brave predator that took on those two. To this day, they remain guard geese at the yard day and night and do a cracking job.

Around the same time, Thelma became unwell. She appeared more grumpy than normal and was obviously struggling with some form of pain. The vet came and antibiotics were administered by injection, which Thelma did not appreciate one bit. She ran away once the needle was stabbed through her thick skin and the vet had to run alongside her to be able to actually thrust all the medication through the needle into her body. I learnt that day how surprisingly fast pigs can run and, how loud they can scream. Poor Thelma.

A ten-day supply of antibiotics was left for Mum to carry on the course. The running on the part of Thelma and the human who had volunteered or been nominated to inject her (Moyà, Cheryl or Mum) got faster as the days went on as Thelma quickly learnt the routine. The screaming got even louder. I felt very sorry for her but kept reminding myself they were trying to help her get better. They managed between them to administer the whole ten-day course, which I thought was quite an achievement as Thelma wasn't the easiest patient. Thelma didn't really seem to pick up though and started to drop weight drastically and be fussy with eating.

Lots of tasty offerings were bought to try and tempt her to eat but she turned her nose up at pretty much everything. Cakes, doughnuts (her favourite) and lots of different breads. I helpfully sampled some of the food for her; it was lovely and delicious, but she didn't want any of it.

Another ten-day course of antibiotics was prescribed. The administering of it got more and more difficult with Thelma anticipating what was going to happen and bulldozing through both Moyà and Mum at different times. Again though, they tried to do what they thought was their best for her.

One day in the middle of June 2021, Thelma collapsed in the yard. Mum spent the whole day trying to help her. She was on the phone to the vet several times and she was willing Thelma to find her feet and get up, but Thelma just couldn't, and, in the end, Mum was convinced by the vet that she had to do the kindest thing. I was taken home in the afternoon and Mum returned to the yard without me. When she came home later that evening, she was very pale and quiet. She didn't talk much and I could tell it had been a harrowing day for her.

The next morning, Thelma was gone. She was no longer suffering but we all felt it, including poor Louise who was now without her sister with whom she had spent her entire life. It was very solemn for a while.

Jane and her babies

Chapter 17
"This Is Why"

Mr Soft and Mr Burns, two of our house cats, turned out to be Nancy's backup. They had started to use random areas around the house other than the litter trays to toilet regularly and Craig was at the end of his tether, tearing out what little hair he had left. "Take them to the yard! "he said. "I've had enough of all the mess." So, in late June 2021, that's what happened.

Like Nancy, they were contained for an initial settling in period and then set loose. Mr Burns as soon as he was given his freedom, was keen to explore his surroundings and fairly quickly became an excellent rat catcher. Mr Soft, not so much.

Mr Soft didn't want to leave the feed shed and didn't really seem himself. After a few days Mum noticed his breathing wasn't right and his heart rate didn't look normal either, so, he was whipped off to the vets for investigative treatment. It was established he likely had asthma (which may have been exacerbated by the environment) and a heart condition. Due to his health issues, it was decided the yard was not a suitable place for him to live. Mr Soft was taken back home to be a house cat and put on long-term medication to manage his heart condition. His breathing settled down fairly quickly once home and he seemed much happier living back indoors. Mum actually thought he might have also been a little depressed at the yard.

Three days later he somehow managed to escape out of the house. Mum went into panic particularly as he was supposed to have medication daily. The kids, Mum and Craig searched the surrounding streets and delivered posters to the houses on those roads in an effort to try and find him.

After two days of him being missing Mum got a phone call from Craig whilst at the yard. I overheard the conversation. Craig explained to Mum that he really thought he had found Mr Soft that morning wandering around the back of the house. He scooped him up, gave him cuddles and promptly headed to the back door with the intention of returning him to the safety of the house.

As he approached the back door "Mr Soft" got unusually fidgety, and once Craig went to open the door, he adopted a rigor mortis-like way of holding his body. Legs were outstretched and rigid as he attempted to make himself wider than the slightly ajar doorway that he found himself suddenly faced with. At this point Craig realised the cat he was trying to force into the house wasn't actually Mr Soft. He was just one of the many black cats that live on our street.

Mum really laughed as Craig relayed the story. It was a welcome brief moment of relief for her from the stress and worry of Mr Soft being missing. Funnily enough that black cat continued to give Craig a wide berth every time he saw him for quite a few months after that "incident".

Five days on, in the middle of the night, Mum and I got woken up by the real Mr Soft meowing outside the back door. He had come home all by himself. He looked happy and well having had no medication for almost a week. That was three years ago and he is still going strong at home without medication.

Mr Burns remains at the yard. He seems very content. He sleeps by day, hunts by night and hassles the humans for cuddles and affection whenever he can. I don't herd him. I have come to the conclusion that cat herding duties are only really necessary in the house. That is actually to my advantage as it enables me to preserve energy for other necessary tasks.

Mr Burns likes to climb up onto the stable block roof quite regularly but isn't very good at getting back down. He seems to forget this. Every time he ventures up there the realisation of the difficulty he has descending eventually returns to him. This results in him performing his own personal rendition of "howling song of despair". Without fail, he does always manage to get down unaided, but we all have to listen to his pitiful song about his avoidable dilemma every...single...time.

One day he was so busy singing away, pretending to be stuck, that he managed to lose his footing. He proceeded to ski down the entire length of the pitched stable roof at quite some pace, landing rather clumsily in a muddy puddle. On his sudden landing, for a moment he adopted his brother's "rabbit caught in headlights" shocked look. He was comforted by way of a towel dry from Mum and a handful of cat biscuits from Moyà which helped him get over his ordeal.

Mr Burns and Nancy quarrel now and then (about nothing) but from watching their interaction of occasional play, occasional scraps (generally instigated by Nancy) and occasional affectionate moments, I think they quite like each other. Together they manage the pest control fairly well. Nancy's responsibility is mice and birds and Mr Burns manages the rats.

Mr Burns and Mr Soft at the yard

Chapter 18
"One Foot In Front of the Other"

We all adjusted to Thelma not being at the yard over time. Louise turned into an even more spoilt pig with delicious treats brought most days for her for a while and lots of attention and conversation given to her which she seemed to love.

The geese were a content bunch of bird brains making lots of loud, happy noises and exploring their surroundings to the maximum. Sometimes it took a fair while to find them at bedtime. They tended to be either in the neighbouring field having a lie down in the long, lush grass or participating in a group swim in the stream.

That summer was hot and all the animals struggled with the heat. The girls would ride the horses first thing to avoid the heat, and whilst they rode I would be secured in a stable as otherwise I was known to set out on my own and join them. I am pretty good at tracking I just follow my nose. Whilst contained in a stable, I would take the opportunity to have a short power nap. I am a light sleeper though and always ready to work, so, as soon as I heard the clip clop of horse hooves returning to the yard, I would start yapping enthusiastically to remind everyone that I was there and ready to resume duties.

There were days where the horses came in for the entire day as it was sweltering in the field with little shelter. They would often sleep in the stables on these days and some of other yard residents would join in with this activity. Not me so much though I tended to be busy working most of the time and this meant I did get very hot on these days. My daily baths were more bearable in the heat. I was still reluctant when it came to bath time but actually found them quite refreshing.

Louise would go and sunbathe in the field from time to time and if anyone approached her she would chat lots at them. She was coping with the loss of her sister better than we all anticipated. Despite the heat it was a content environment, and, for a few months, there was no drama whatsoever.

Diva and Flynn

Chapter 19
"I'll Be There For You"

Early September, Heidi decided she didn't want her food. Mum wasn't too concerned. It had been quite warm and sometimes that put some of the animals off eating. However, a few days later, Mum got a phone call from Moyà and Cheryl whilst they were at the yard. They hadn't seen Heidi that afternoon.

Heidi had stopped going to bed with the geese some months ago and, since then, had just found her own comfortable place to sleep overnight. It wasn't therefore essential to locate her. Mum told them not to worry and that we would all look for her in the morning.

When Mum and I arrived at the yard the next morning the first thing we all did was search for Heidi. We found her on the edge of the woods lying down. She looked ok but Mum called the vet anyway. Going to hide in the woods coupled with the no eating was enough to warrant a vet visit.

The vet came and there were mutterings of possible liver failure or liver disease, but some medication was administered to see if it would help her get better. Sadly, it didn't. Heidi didn't want to play with me anymore, and she didn't want to follow her goose friends, she just wanted to lie down a lot. I went and lay down with her to see if that would help her get better. It didn't. A day later, just before bedtime, she collapsed and could not get back up. The vet came again, and, that night Heidi went peacefully to sleep.

That was the end of just over a year together, her three years of living at the yard and her approximate fourteen years of life. I feel very sad that Heidi is no longer with us at the yard. She was a nice friend to have and I will miss her deeply for the rest of my life.

Heidi and Flynn

Chapter 20
"Better Way to Live"

Aside from the usual routine at the yard where it would be work, work, work then brief power nap whilst the girls went out for a ride then back to work, there were occasions where we went on road trips together in the horsebox. These were known as "training" outings and were either at the local equestrian centre or Mum's friend Ann's yard. I enjoyed travelling in the car. The horse box was just as good if not a better experience. The cargo would be two horses, at least two girls (where at least one of them was Mum) and me.

The equestrian centre was only a few miles from the yard so the journey there was fairly brief. On arrival I would be tethered to limit my herding service whilst the girls rode mostly round and round in circles and sometimes over some obstacles. As I was not free enough to complete my herding service to my usual excellent standard I would weave side to side with the occasional yelp to assist with motivation and movement. For some reason this wasn't appreciated and Mum would regularly say, "Calm down Flynn, we don't need your help." I was only doing my job so mostly ignored what she said and continued to provide occasional barks in assistance as and when I considered them necessary.

When we went to Ann's it was a longer journey so I would have a sleep on the way so that I was refreshed and ready for duty on arrival. Ann was different to any of the other humans I knew. Older and wiser, for a start. She came across as quite stern, but she wasn't. It was a slightly different agenda to that at the equestrian centre when we went to Ann's place.

Ann had a young golden Labrador called Major, and when we went there I had the privilege of running around the horse enclosure and playing with him before the "training" began. Major was a bit bolshy and clumsy. Initially I was a bit dubious about joining in with his rather boisterous-like efforts at play, but eventually he convinced me that it might be fun to bound around a bit and have friendly brief wrestles together. Our playtime was never extensively long but it was nice to have a non-work activity with a goofy new friend for a brief moment. The girls and Ann seemed to enjoy watching us run around together.

The training sessions at Ann's were varied. Some involved lots of movement from the horses and the girls where (although tethered) I would again assist with yelps at appropriate moments. Some sessions didn't require much movement at all and I couldn't really work out what anyone was doing other than standing around and talking lots. During this type of session I would provide intense supervision and make sure everyone stayed in line.

There was clearly success in achieving objectives set for both types of training sessions as there were outbursts now and then from Ann of, "Yes, that's it! You've got it!" She was very encouraging and positive, and I could feel that Mum and the girls had a lot of respect, admiration and time for her. The time that we all spent there was happy. There was lots of laughter, smiles and learning.

The end of the training sessions always went the same way. Mum would say, "We have to get off now." Ann would acknowledge that we needed to leave but talk and talk and talk some more. The girls obviously loved listening to what she had to say and spending time with her, but Mum always had to shoehorn us all away with the final words of, "We really have to go now, Ann" where Ann would reply, "Oh sorry love, yes of course." Leaving was always delayed by a few minutes but despite this the feelings towards Ann were always positive and caring. There was never any resentment for the mandatory few minutes delay.

Mum came away from the sessions with Ann feeling that another building block in her knowledge of horsemanship had been provided, and we all looked forward to the next visit. I heard Mum say on more than one occasion that she considered Ann the best horsewoman she had ever met and regarded her as a true and good friend.

Diva, Gertsje, Flynn and Julie

Chapter 21
"Part of the Band"

The yard felt very empty without Heidi. Losing her left a huge hole in all our hearts. During her time at the yard she had gone from feral to tame and from an animal that would simply run away from everyone to a brave, demanding, spoilt and funny old goat. We missed her greeting us at the gate in the mornings scouting for any treats that may have been brought for her. We missed her turning her nose up at certain offerings by butting gently the hand offering the "unsatisfactory" food item as if saying "I'm not eating that rubbish." We missed her butting the feed bins in a demand to be fed. We missed her following around her goose friends. We missed her matador games. I felt a bit lost and sad without her to play with, and Mum felt that. It was decided the yard needed at least one goat. The search was on.

From what I heard there were plenty of goats to choose from, but Mum took her time and found two Golden Guernsey brothers that she considered would be great additions to the yard family. They were to be called Fred and Ginger. Mum spent two days fencing a suitable area for them to live in, and Craig built them a goat shed. They joined us in October.

The day they came was interesting. Mum collected them in the horsebox and once they were unloaded at the yard, they proceeded to walk straight through all the electric fencing that she had spent so long erecting. Despite the electric fence being on and delivering multiple electric shocks to them, they didn't care and it didn't deter them. They just leisurely walked through the fencing time and time again and went wherever they wanted to go.

They are incredibly tame and much larger than Heidi. They also look a bit funny. Their "funny look" is due to them both having been badly dehorned when they were very young resulting in their horns being somewhat deformed. Fred looks like a unicorn and Ginger looks like he is wearing an oversized snail shell on his head. Nevertheless they are lovely natured.

Fred was quite nervous when they arrived and was constantly looking for his brother and hiding behind him. He had to always have Ginger in his sight, otherwise he would have a bit of a panic. Ginger was much more confident. I was very wary of them both initially. They were much taller than me and I considered they could and might hurt me. They were fairly interested in me though and kept slowly approaching. I just kept increasing the distance between us, just to be sure.

When they had finished demolishing all the electric fencing, they noticed the goat shed and went and settled down inside it. Despite the lack of electric fencing to contain them, they made no effort to leave the confines of the yard. They seemed quite comfortable and happy, and remain so.

Fred has grown in confidence and now no longer hides behind his brother. He also does not worry if Ginger is out of sight. They, like everyone else at the yard, get lots of treats brought for them by Moya. They love ginger biscuits and bread (as Heidi did). They are always inquisitive of any bags that are brought into the yard in case they harbour tasty food items. They play between themselves butting heads, running around the field together and flinging themselves around.

Fred is the naughtiest and often gets told off for pinching things out of bags or coat pockets. Ginger is better behaved and cuddlier, but both of them enjoy a brush and attention. Fred is more vocal than Ginger and when he gets shouted at by Mum for being naughty, he answers back with a cute, almost apologetic, bleating.

I am less wary of both of them now. I think it was their size and the way they looked that intimidated me. They both went through a stage of stealing food out of the feed shed but Mum and I managed to put a stop to that. Mum would shout "Get out of there!" I would back her up by charging into the feed room and evicting them by way of ankle nipping. It was, and remains, a very effective method of moving livestock.

They are obviously lovely friendly inquisitive creatures, but, they are not Heidi. I have yet to play matador games with either of them, but Mum is hopeful that it might happen one day.

Moya and Ginger

Chapter 22
"Leave Me Alone"

After a few months of us all getting into the swing of the winter yard routine again, there was to be a new arrival. A friend for Louise, called Wilma. We all thought that it would be nice for Louise to have a piggy friend that she could cuddle up to again during the cold winter months. We also imagined she would appreciate the company having been without her sister Thelma for about six months. Wilma arrived the day before Christmas Eve, and instead of it being a fairy tale meeting it was very much the opposite, loud and very traumatic, especially for poor Louise.

Louise innocently approached Wilma to say "Hello" and Wilma took immediate offence and viciously attacked her. She pushed her into a ditch and took a chunk out of her with her large strong teeth. Louise tried to run to the safety of her pig pen but Wilma was determined and decided that the pig pen now belonged to her and Louise was not allowed anywhere near it. Louise was banished by Wilma to the farthest point of the yard and there she stayed overnight, taking shelter from the rain under a tree. It was a very sorry sight, and not what anyone at the yard had expected would happen on the introduction of a new friend.

Mum went on an emergency shopping trip and bought Louise a new pig arc which was shoehorned into the back of the 4x4, transported to the yard, and then subsequently erected so that by the time the sun set on Christmas Eve, Louise had a new pig house in a new location.

Unsurprisingly after her ordeal Louise stayed far away from Wilma and the rest of the yard for a while. She was provided with food and water in her new living quarters, but after a week or so she started to bravely venture back towards the yard. Whilst carefully sauntering up towards the yard, every time she sensed Wilma was near, she would scream and run off in fear. This went on for a couple more weeks. Wilma never gave the impression she would attack again, but Louise was obviously very concerned that she might.

Less than four weeks after Wilma arrived, Louise and Wilma started to be friends. It began with gentle sniffing and just walking calmly past each other, and then it didn't take very long for them to bond and become inseparable. It was a huge relief and rather heart-warming after such a stressful start. Louise and Wilma spent the rest of that winter cuddled up happily together. They never fought (not even for food) and were very content with each other for company.

Besties Wilma and Louise

Chapter 23
"Cruel Summer"

Mating season came around again in the following spring but this time, as there were plenty of girls for the three ganders, there was very little fighting amongst the geese. The Krays still had a go at everyone else in the yard though, including the new goats. There was, however, one animal on the yard that they didn't attack. That was Wilma. They would make a beeline for Louise and give her a real battering (she would scream and run away) but never once did they chase or bite Wilma. All the geese seemed to be happy in their large gaggle of eight and wandered the confines of the yard fairly amicably together. Mum did have to remove eggs from under the females now and then. This fuelled The Krays hatred and diabolical behaviour as they were very passionate about their guarding job.

We sadly lost two young female geese that spring. One had been sitting and Mr Fox had snatched her (how he got past The Krays is a mystery to as all). All that remained of her was one wing. The other goose became ill quite suddenly. Mum rushed to the vet and got and administered medication immediately, but when we arrived the next morning, she had died overnight. I saw Mum cry when she buried her. It was sad to lose the two baby geese.

The two remaining female geese got named Bendy (because her neck is a kind of "S" shape and therefore "bendy") and Wendy (simply because it rhymes with bendy.) Even though the boys had lost two girlfriends, Bendy, Wendy and Jane seemed enough to keep the three boys occupied and happy.

Louise sadly became unwell in the summer. We all knew what was coming. The girls tried their best with their Florence Nightingale efforts. Louise was brought yummy treats and for a while she humoured the offerings and, briefly, ate small amounts. Eventually, though, just like her sister, she didn't want to eat anything at all, no matter how delicious it might be. This was sad to see, especially for a pig that used to sing a happy pig song whilst chewing through her meals. She had been such a lovely, happy, funny pig. We all wanted her to stay that way and remain with us forever.

The inevitable came sooner than we all hoped. She outlived her sister by thirteen months and, despite an initial hiccup, had had a lovely new companion for the last six months or so of her life. We would all miss her. The girls would miss her chatty personality and her willingness to be letterbox fed when it came to bread and cake. I would miss sharing her snacks and moving her around by gently nipping her ankles. The Krays would miss bullying her. Wilma would miss her one, and only, pig friend. R.I.P Louise.

Louise

Chapter 24
"Lil Boo Thang"

Life went on at Paradise Club as it always does, and in the spring of 2023 at home, a new animal face appeared uninvited. Our road has always had a high population of cats which is most obvious at night time when you can hear evidence of the various territorial street brawls.

A young male black cat with striking white markings started spending time in an empty planter in our front garden. Over a short period of time it kind of became his daily hang out. Our front garden can be quite the sun trap, and, we would find this handsome cat regularly curled up in the planter soaking up the sun. Mum and I would see him when leaving or returning to the house. He always looked very comfortable and at home (even though it wasn't his official home).

Over the months the time he would stay in the planter seemed to increase and there were occasions when, if he wasn't in the front garden, that you might find him around the back of the house occupying our balcony area or perched on the kitchen windowsill. Anyone could be forgiven for thinking he was our cat. He has, however, never been officially part of our family nor has he ever lived with us despite his best efforts.

His home is directly across the road from us where he is most welcome and has been known to visit on occasion.

The time he spends in our front garden has increased even more over the last year. He now sleeps in the planter in our front porch area most days and actually most nights too. Mum has put a couple of blankets in there to keep him warm and comfortable.

He greets me and Mum every morning when we leave the house with a lovely "meow" to say hello followed by mandatory leg rubs for us both. He then follows us to the garage and waves us off as we leave to go to the yard for the morning. When we return later in the day it's not unusual for him to be in the planter.

I have noticed that he does some quite exemplary escorting duties. As well as walking us to the car every morning, he sometimes follows the kids almost all the way to the bus stop and the local shop. He has also been known to join Bella and me when we go for walks on The Killacourt.

He guards the front garden, greeting any human visitors and ensuring neighbouring cats do not pass the threshold. We hear or see him having heated altercations with some of the many cats that live on the street whilst he carries out his guarding duty. He initially adopts verbal persuasion methods with the cat intruders, backed up with physical force as and when necessary. He obviously considers the front garden HIS territory and they must not enter.

He has become a very lovely handsome garden feature either snuggled in the planter, sat neatly on the gas metre box beside the front door, wandering in the back garden or perched on the kitchen windowsill.

On occasion he manages to sneak in through the front door when people come to visit, and don't realise that he's not our cat. They mistakenly let him follow them in when entering the house. He does get ousted fairly promptly once Mum spots him casually strolling around inside the house. "What's this cat doing in our house?" she will say. The reply is always, "Sorry, I thought he lived here." What follows is laughter and, "Don't worry, so does he."

Keanu is a beautiful, handsome, vocal, affectionate, obsessive, feline stalker and a welcome addition to our lives, albeit by constant gate-crash.

Keanu

Chapter 25
"Feather"

Over the years Mum would occasionally be assigned the task of looking after chickens that lived in the garden of the house opposite the yard. It was essentially holiday cover whilst the owner went away for a few weeks. The girls would help Mum with this task but I wasn't allowed to provide assistance, which was disappointing from my perspective. I would be contained in one of the stables whilst the girls carried out these "chicken duties". This was, apparently, for my own safety. There were always stories when the girls returned from these duties.

Four chickens and a rooster resided next door. None of the girls seemed to know whether the chickens or the rooster had official names, but as time went on the rooster acquired and earnt the nickname of "Ninja". This was due to the lightning speed with which he could pursue and attack with precision. Very quickly whenever going to do chicken duties, a plastic shovel would be taken for protection.

According to Mum, Moya, Cheryl and Julie, Ninja was not friendly. This, actually, was a massive understatement. They all agreed that he made The Krays look tame by comparison. He was violent, aggressive and unpleasant, but, what made him a particularly difficult character to manage was his unpredictability. Generally, if the geese were going to attack, you would get a bit of a warning.

Ninja, however, liked to operate with a constant element of surprise.

One might imagine that perhaps his behaviour was merely because he was protecting his girlfriends. No, that wasn't the case. He was also extremely unpleasant to his doting females, illustrating his unpredictability and vicious tendencies by giving any one of them a severe pecking quite regularly out of the blue. One of the hens seemed to be the main recipient of his regular violent outbursts. She, physically, looked quite haggard and was missing quite a few feathers due to his almost constant abuse of her.

Ninja's method of assault for his girlfriends was charge, then corner and peck away severely. You couldn't even say there was a pecking order. It was just him well and truly at the top and all the hens doing their best to try and not do anything that riled him, which by the looks of it could be as little as turning their heads the wrong way, walking in the wrong direction or breathing. He was the ultimate definition of nasty. An unreasonable, power hungry loud mouth who felt the need to constantly throw his weight around and beat everyone up.

His attacks on Mum, Moya, Cheryl and Julie were similar to those of his chicken companions, but the build-up to the charge seemed a bit more calculated. Ninja would quietly give the impression that he was just minding his own business, walking around, perhaps casually pecking the floor in a fairly relaxed manner whilst giving the impression he was busily occupied. This would be so that whichever of the girls who was on duty that day might let their guard down and perhaps even lower the shovel from the protective shield-like position. The charge would commence at the most unexpected moment and would crescendo into a very determined body launch with claws outstretched ready to stab into the legs of his victim. His behaviour, manner and attitude were diabolical.

Whenever chicken duty was completed by whichever of the girls had been "volunteered", there would always be the same question of them on return to the yard "Did Ninja get you?" To begin with the answer was more times than not "Yes." As time went on, however, all of the girls did get better at defending themselves, meaning that the shovel would then take the brunt of his attacks.

Despite managing the Ninja gatekeeper, Mum and the girls did enjoy looking after the chickens and they did miss it when holiday cover ceased. There was only one thing for it. We needed some chickens of our own.

Flynn, Corgan, Ginger, Mr Burns, Nancy and me

Chapter 26
"Spit of You"

The first of our chicken residents was a rooster. Mum wasn't looking for a rooster really, particularly considering the ordeals she had endured with Ninja but whilst scouring the internet for chickens for sale the advert for this little man couldn't be ignored. He was an eight-week-old Silkie cross Wellsummer. Very much under his mother's wing and still looking to sleep snuggled under her every night. He came and was really quite small but Mum nurtured him. She handled him a lot and told him it wouldn't be long before he had company. He would be placed in the feed shed whilst she made up feeds in the morning so he had some form of company and interaction each day.

A week later he was joined by two young Silkie hens; one golden in colour and the other pure black. The trio were named Zuko, Sandy and Rizzo. They lived in a shed by night and had a secure outside enclosure where they would spend time in the day, weather permitting. I felt they required a considerable amount of intense supervision from me. I could spend literally hours watching them and making sure their behaviour was acceptable. They seemed to behave very well but, perhaps if I didn't supervise so intensely, that might not remain the case.

Zuko blossomed into a beautiful friendly rooster and his two girlfriends seemed quite happy with him as company with Sandy always by his side and Rizzo not far behind. Rizzo was more independent and perhaps a little bit of a gooseberry at times. Mum often picked them all up together to transport them to and from their outside enclosure and when she did this I would do my best to remain very close to them and her ensuring that Mum transported them efficiently.

They were chatty, funny-looking birds and didn't seem too bothered with my presence although they weren't particularly comfortable if I put my nose right next to them when Mum was holding them. I would get told to go lie down and stop bothering them if Mum considered I was upsetting them. They lived quite happily together between the shed and the enclosure for a while.

We had a few stormy days in November 2023 and one morning (after a very rough stormy night) when Mum and I arrived and opened the shed to check on them, Sandy had sadly died. Mum thought she might have had a heart attack. Zuko was stood over her as if waiting for her to get up. It was both sad and touching. One rooster and one hen didn't seem enough on their own so three days later there were three more chicken additions. Three new bantam girlfriends for Zuko named Alice, Tweedledee and Tweedledum. Zuko was so excited to meet them that he did a little song and dance when they were introduced. It was both sweet and funny. They, Rizzo and Zuko are an incredibly happy bunch together. There are lots of very chatty happy noises that come from them all the time.

Zuko doesn't bully any of the girls. He is not at all aggressive and has a lovely soft nature. He is the tamest out of all of them. Mum can easily catch him whereas all the girls give her a bit of a chicken run around. He likes a cuddle and a stroke and he sometimes comes into the yard and helps with supervision whilst the girls muck out. His supervision skills aren't as good as mine, obviously. I, therefore, supervise him whilst he's supervising the girls to make sure everything is done to a good standard. I juggle this task with supervising the hens in their enclosure at the same time which involves me running back and forth to ensure equal amounts of time are allocated to both extremely important supervisory tasks. It works pretty well although I do sometimes get told off for trying to trip up the girls as, apparently, I don't always look where I'm running.

Zuko is pretty noisy. Every time he does his noisy call I have to run over to wherever he might be and make sure he is adhering to acceptable standards of behaviour. To date he has not put a foot wrong but, you never know. He is a rooster after all so I need to keep a close eye on him. We wouldn't want him turning into another Ninja would we?

Flynn, Zuko, Rizzo, Alice, Tweedledum and Tweedledee

Chapter 27
"Harder Better Faster Stronger"

I'm four years old now; older but some would say not wiser. I live a very busy but happy life. My days always start off with a touch of cat herding and dancing and then I head off in the car to the yard with Mum where I am incredibly happy. I ride shotgun and have my own seatbelt. I wag my tail in appreciation as we approach the gate just to let Mum know how content I am, and, also as a sign of gratitude.

My energy levels at the yard are full to bursting. I am "super dog" at the yard; ready for anything. My role there is varied and extremely important. I am the busiest most hard-working and efficient worker on the yard. Officially I am foreman, worker and supervisor all at the same time.

I regularly remind everyone at the yard of my importance and authority by way of high-pitched yelping delivered at random and multiple intervals of time whilst spinning in circles. I'm actually singing my favourite work song which goes, "Work harder, better, faster, stronger, work harder, better, faster, stronger, work harder, better, faster, stronger." Some might describe it as a bit repetitive but I consider it helps motivate everyone to try and do as good a job as me.

Mum doesn't seem to enjoy my song very much particularly when it gets extremely high-pitched whereupon I'm told to "pack it in" and encouraged into a stable to "lie down and calm down" for a few minutes. Thankfully these forced intervals are brief and I'm released fairly promptly to start again with building momentum in my circles and volume and pitch in my work song.

My time at the yard is mainly spent herding and supervising. I herd the horses, goats, geese (from a distance and not in mating season) and Wilma. I enjoy herding Wilma the most particularly whilst she is eating breakfast. I am fairly proud that I can actually get her to run away from her food at quite some pace whilst squealing but chewing the small mouthful she has managed to snatch.

According to Mum I should leave Wilma alone whilst she is eating but the only other time I get to herd her is when she makes herself comfortable in the goats shed (which is out of bounds for her). That doesn't happen very often so breakfast time is my only regular opportunity to herd her and I take it willingly.

My main supervision responsibility is that of the chickens. This requires a very high level of concentration. I don't even blink when carrying out this duty. Some might describe my supervising skills as a little intense but I'm of the view that if a job is worth doing, it's worth doing well.

I help fill the water buckets in the morning by running around in circles and offering high-pitched yelps of encouragement. I help fill the haynets by running around in circles and offering high-pitched yelps of encouragement. I help muck out by running around in circles and offering high-pitched yelps of encouragement. I help turn out the horses by running around in circles and offering high-pitched yelps of encouragement. I help myself to cat biscuits out of the cat's bowl in the feed shed when no one is looking. Also, Moyà quite often brings a bag of treats (which aren't generally meant for me). I help myself to those treats too when the opportunity arises.

When all the morning work at the yard is complete I reluctantly have a bath (which is more thorough if I've rolled in fox poo) and head back home to resume herding duties of the cats for a few hours. Later, when we return to the yard, I go for a walk with Craig whilst Mum puts the animals to bed. I then go home again for a final shift of cat herding, a little bit of house guarding with Bella (when we provide our doggy doorbell song service) a final dog walk and then it's time to rest.

My favourite resting place is underneath Mum's recliner in the front room. It is a slight inconvenience to her that I choose this as my primary resting spot as every time Mum tries to get up from her seat I'm in the way. She has to ask me to move to enable her to be able to rise from her seat. It doesn't deter me from lying there though, and, to be honest I don't think she really minds too much.

I'm exhausted by the end of the day but feel very fulfilled with the standard of workmanship I constantly deliver and how much I achieve each day. I sleep like a baby and wake the next morning full of beans and ready to go again.

I love my life and feel very lucky. I get to spend every day with a variety of animal and human companions, mostly in the great outdoors. I feel privileged in my friendships past and present. It's been sad to lose friends along the way, but Mum says that is part of life and that we should think of them often and cherish our memories. That way they stay with us forever.

I have already had a fair share of experiences and adventures in my short four years of life. No doubt there will be many more ahead and I'm ready for them with my friends beside me. Thank you for reading about my life. I hope you have enjoyed sharing the experiences as much as I have enjoyed living them.

Cheryl, Danny and Flynn

Epilogue
"Took a While"

When I started writing this book about four years ago, I soon lost motivation and it came to a grinding halt. The inspiration to write again came from the loss of my close friend Ann a few months ago. The almost indescribable feeling of grief led to a surge of overwhelming inspiration to write. I found that writing helped me feel less bereft. I therefore have Ann to thank for helping me finish writing it.

I wasn't initially sure how the book was going to pan out. My other two novels have definitive plots. Bella's was about being lost and then found and Fudge's book was about his entire life. Flynn's not been lost and found and is only four years old so in order for the book to be about his whole life I would potentially be writing it for another ten or more years which would never be the plan. My dilemma was therefore what would the point, plot or purpose be of Flynn's book? It took me a while to work that it was to be about life experiences, adventures and friendship and all the real true feelings that are entwined into all of that. How fortunate are Flynn and I to have experienced all these moments together surrounded by the support and love of our friends?

As there has been loss of a few of our friends during the 'lifetime' of this book I have been forced to face and express feelings and emotions surrounding those losses which I think has also helped me understand and deal with my grieving process. I have found it difficult to write and revisit those losses but can't help thinking that writing about it has been like some form of therapy for me.

Pretty much all of the stories and adventures that are set out in this book were relayed to Ann before she died and she shared the mixture of emotions with me that each episode brought. I loved talking to her about everything and anything and I do miss not be able to do that anymore.

I always want to deliver perfection when I write. I have literally spent hours and hours creating and editing this book but I am still not convinced that it is as good as it should be. Hopefully, however, you have enjoyed reading it. It's been my absolute pleasure to write down Flynn's story and I do hope I have made Ann proud.

Flynn and Corgan

Milton Keynes UK
Ingram Content Group UK Ltd.
UKHW022200240424
441687UK00013B/446